GLENMORE VALLEY

A Rosette for Maeve?

Anna McQuinn

Illustrated by Paul Young

NEWHAM LIBRARIES

The voice of Ireland's farming industry
www.farmersjournal.ie
IRISH FARMERS JOURNAL

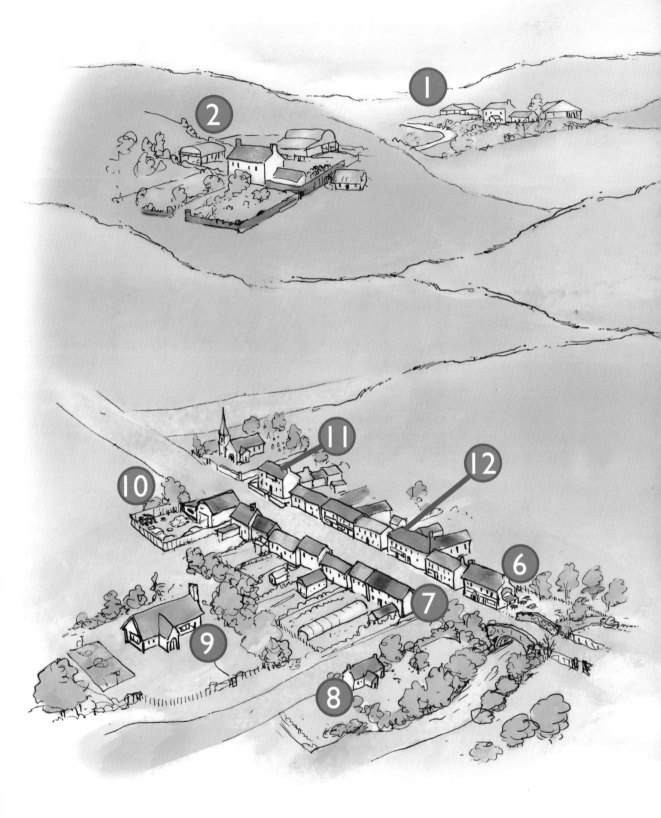

THE FARMS

1 O'SULLIVANS' BEEF FARM

2 REIDYS' DAIRY FARM

3 FITZGERALDS' STUD FARM

4 O'CONNORS' SHEEP FARM

5 LISTONS' SHEEP FARM

THE VILLAGE

6 THE ICE-CREAM PARLOUR

7 CAFFREYS' CAFÉ

8 VET GERALDINE BROSNAN'S HOUSE

9 NAOMH BRID NATIONAL SCHOOL

10 CLIFFORDS' GARAGE

11 O'SHEAS' B&B

12 FARM-RELIEF MAN ANTHONY COLLINS'S HOUSE

First published 2013 by The O'Brien Press Ltd
12 Terenure Road East, Rathgar,
Dublin 6, Ireland,
Tel: +353 1 4923333; Fax: +353 1 4922777
E-mail: books@obrien.ie.
Website: www.obrien.ie
Published in association with the Irish Farmers Journal

ISBN: 978-1-84717-340-9

1 2 3 4 5 6 7 8
13 14 15 16 17 18

Printed by EDELVIVES, Spain
The paper in this book is produced using pulp from managed
forests

THE PEOPLE

CIARAN AND NIAMH REIDY live on a dairy farm. Ciaran is 7. His best friend is Seán Clifford. Niamh is 9. Her best friend is Lisa O'Sullivan. Their mum also runs holiday cottages on the farm so there's always lots to do, and Ciaran and Niamh have to help out.

MEGAN, HANNAH AND CARMEL MAHER are cousins of Ciaran and Niamh. They run an ice-cream parlour in the village selling ice-cream they make themselves (along with yoghurt).

LISA AND JOE O'SULLIVAN live on a beef farm. Their dad raises prize-winning cattle and he is also a teacher in Glenmore National School. Lisa is 9 and is very good at knitting. Joe is only 3.

SEÁN AND TOMÁS CLIFFORD are twins, aged 8. Their dad is a local tradesman. Everyone loves to go to play at their house because their garage is so full of great stuff for making forts or houses, and their older brother is cool. They like to go to their friends' houses, but they are always getting into trouble.

MOLLY AND DAISY CAFFREY moved to the village from Dublin. Their family runs Nourish, a café in the village. Molly is 7 and Daisy is 4. They love art and making things.

COLM AND MICHAEL O'CONNOR live on a sheep farm. Colm is 8 and is great at football. He plays on the local Glenmore Ramblers team. He wants to be a farmer and own horses when he is grown up. Michael is 7 and is into dinosaurs, and goes nowhere without his dinosaur, Screechy.

ANTHONY COLLINS is the Farm-Relief man and **GERALDINE BROSNAN** is the vet. She is a regular visitor to the farms and has three dogs called Ratty, Scruffy and Scratchy.

Hi!

My name is Lisa O'Sullivan.

I live on a beef farm with my three-year-old brother, Joe,

and my mum and dad.

I am nine and my favourite subject at school is art.

My family is busy getting ready for

the Glenmore Valley Show.

Dad is going to show his bull, Samson,

and Mum is busy making cakes –

one for the cake competition and some for

the cupcake stand.

All the mums are making cupcakes and the money is going

to help buy new jerseys for the Under-12 football team.

And this year I'm doing something new and special.

I'm so nervous!

The Glenmore Valley Show is on in a few days' time. The farmers will show their best animals, and there are competitions for arts and crafts and baking and fashion. Everyone in the valley will enter something. But everyone is keeping their entry a secret, so there's a great buzz of excitement and mystery around the valley.

★ ★ ★

Lisa O'Sullivan was waiting at the school gate with her friend, Niamh Reidy.

'So, how are your projects going, Niamh?' she asked. (Even though the entries were all secret, everyone was dying to know how their friends were getting on.)

'My recycling one is done and my art one just needs a few finishing touches,' said Niamh. 'What about yours?'

'I'm only doing one – an art project,' said Lisa.

'But you won two prizes last year! Why aren't you doing a knitting one?'

'I'm doing something else,' said Lisa, 'but I can't talk about it.' She waved as her dad drove up. 'Sorry, I have to go. See you tomorrow.'

Lisa's secret was that her dad had asked her to show their new calf in the calf competition. He had always shown his cattle, but this was the first calf they'd bred on the farm. She was a Belgian Blue, and she had a white coat with blue-grey patches on it. Lisa's dad had let her choose the name too. Lisa decided on Maeve, after the famous Queen Maeve who loved cattle. Lisa would have to walk the calf around the show ring, then stand still while Maeve was being judged.

Young calves don't like being led around in a halter, so Lisa began her training a whole month before the show. First, she put a halter on Maeve for half an hour every day to let the little calf get used to the idea. Once Maeve got used to the halter, Lisa began to walk her around in a circle.

At first Lisa had to pull hard to get Maeve to move at all. Then when Maeve suddenly decided to cooperate, she leapt forward and crashed into Lisa! Lisa fell over with a bump.

'Oh, you silly thing,' she said, rubbing her bum. 'That *hurt!*'

'And it's *not* funny!' she shouted at her brother, Joe, who was giggling nearby.

'Joe do it!' said Joe.

Lisa was about to say no, but then felt that Joe could help. She gave him a small stick and as Lisa pulled Maeve along, Joe gave the calf a little tap now and then from behind.

After a lot of practice, Maeve followed Lisa around beautifully.

'Looking good, Missy,' said Lisa's dad when he came to see how she was getting on.

'She's nearly ready for the catwalk, Dad,' smiled Lisa.

'Well, next up you must train her to stand still,' said Dad, 'because the judges want to get a good long look. And you must get her to hold her head up nice and high, so she looks her absolute best.'

But it was very hard to get Maeve to stand still. Every time Lisa got her to stop, three seconds later Maeve was off again.

'Oh no!' scolded Lisa. 'You must stand or we won't get any marks!'

'Just be patient,' advised Dad, 'you're nearly there.' Then he added, 'Do you think she's ready for a makeover?'

'A what?'

'Well, a little trim of her coat, and a hairwash,' replied Dad. 'She's not dirty right now, but it's good to get her used to it rather than wait until too near the show.'

'Actually, I think she'll love it,' said Lisa. 'She thinks she's a top model, you know!'

'Will she want something fancy, then, or do you think she'll be okay with the show shampoo?' smiled Dad.

'We'll just do a small bit today and let her get used to the idea,' he said. 'Now, hold her steady.'

But Maeve wriggled and shifted around. It was quite hard to clip her hair.

'She's trying to look back to see what you're doing!' giggled Lisa. 'I think we should get a mirror!'

'And maybe a few magazines!' laughed Dad.

'And give her a cappuchino!' said Lisa.

'She's a bit demanding, isn't she?' said Dad.

'Well, she *is* hoping to be Glenmore's next top calf-model!' said Lisa.

Lisa and her dad poured warm water on Maeve's back and Lisa rubbed in some shampoo. Then they rinsed everything off and rubbed Maeve down with an old towel.

'She's still a bit damp,' said Lisa.

'Ah, she'll dry off in no time,' said Dad.

A few days later, Lisa was doing her homework when her dad put a package in front of her. Lisa looked at him curiously.

'Go on, open it,' he said. 'It's a surprise.'

Lisa carefully folded back the brown paper. It was a white coat – a smaller version of the one Dad wore when he showed his cattle. It had their family crest and 'O'Sullivan's Farm' in small letters on it.

'You've done a real professional job getting Maeve ready,' explained Dad. 'So I thought you should look the part too.'

'It's brilliant, Dad, thanks,' said Lisa. She ran to the mirror to try it on.

It was perfect.

With only a day to go, Glenmore Valley was buzzing. After school, Lisa ran outside for one last practice. Maeve had finally learned to stand still, yet Lisa struggled every time.

'Dad – I think maybe you should handle Maeve yourself tomorrow. I'm afraid she won't stand for me.'

'Sweetheart, we all had a first time,' said Dad, 'and, sure, if you make a mistake, what harm. That's how you learn. As long as you do your best, that's all that matters.'

'Thanks, Dad. But you won two rosettes with the cattle last year. I don't want you to lose one for our first calf just because I can't make Maeve stand still,' said Lisa.

'Well, you've done all the hard work with her, so she's more likely to behave for you than for anyone else,' replied Dad. 'And I know you'll do well.'

The O'Sullivans were up bright and early on Saturday. Lisa and Dad went to the shed to prepare the show box.

'Here,' said Dad. 'I've got something extra special for the supermodel!'

Lisa read the label and laughed: 'Styling wax?'

'You rub it in just before you show her, for that extra bit of shine!' said Dad.

'Because she's worth it!' giggled Lisa.

After breakfast they loaded the animals in their two trailers. Lisa's mum drove one car and her dad the other. By half-past nine they'd found their space in the preparation area behind the show ring. Lisa settled Maeve in, while Dad looked after Samson.

'I'm meeting Niamh to look around, is that okay?' Lisa asked.

'That's fine,' said Mum. 'I'll stay here while Dad takes Joe to see the tractors. Then I'm going to look around myself.'

'Don't be too late back. The calf competition starts at two o'clock,' warned Dad.

Lisa met up with Niamh and they walked around the craft tent together.

'Oh, look, I've got a first! The red rosette!' squealed Niamh, pointing at her picture.

'Well done!' said Lisa, hugging her friend. She looked around for her own picture and was disappointed there was no rosette.

'I can't believe you didn't get one,' said Niamh. 'Your picture is brilliant. You *always* win something.'

'Molly Caffrey got second – actually, her picture's pretty good,' admitted Lisa.

'And look! Tomás Clifford got third,' said Niamh. 'I think his is rubbish,' she added in a whisper, hugging her friend loyally. 'You should have won.'

It's all down to Maeve now, thought Lisa to herself.

It was very quiet in the food tent. There was a cookery demonstration on.

'That's that fellow off the telly,' whispered Lisa.

'I think he ate too many of his own cakes,' giggled Niamh. 'Hey, look. Molly's mother's cake is amazing! She's got first.'

'She does the baking for her café, so she's brilliant,' said Lisa. 'Look at all those sweets!' she said, pointing to another cake.

'No one will miss one – or two!' said Niamh, picking two carefully off the back of the cake and handing one to Lisa. 'Come on! Let's get out of here.'

One of the most exciting things at the show was the sheepdog competition. It was Lisa and Niamh's favourite, so they made their way to the central arena. Niamh's brother, Ciaran, and his best friend, Seán Clifford and his brother, Tomás, were already there. So were Chris, Colm and Molly from school.

'Are you really disappointed you didn't get a prize for your picture?' asked Niamh. 'You always win something.'

'I am a bit.' Lisa couldn't keep her secret to herself anymore. 'But I have a special thing happening today,' she said. 'My dad asked me to handle Maeve in the calf competition.'

'That's brilliant!' said Niamh.

'Wow!' said Chris. 'I wish my dad would allow me to handle one of ours.'

'Isn't it dangerous?' asked Molly.

'Maeve is only five months old,' said Lisa. 'The only real trouble is getting her to stand still.'

'She's still fairly strong,' said Tomás. 'If she decided to run off, you couldn't catch her. You're only a girl.'

'Girls are just as strong as boys,' said Niamh, giving Tomás an elbow and knocking him off the bale of straw.

'I'm going to cheer for Lisa! She's the only one in our whole school in the competition,' said Niamh.

'Me too!' said Molly.

'And me!' said Colm. 'I hope she beats all the grown ups.'

'Maybe if you win, my dad will allow me in it next year,' said Chris. 'I'll come to cheer too.'

'But isn't your dad *in* the calf competition?' asked Niamh.

'Oh, yes, I forgot!' said Chris. 'Maybe he can come second.'

Lisa headed off to the preparation area. She put on her white coat.

'Mum, I need the loo – right now!' she whispered.

'You're just nervous, love. Come on, I'll come with you,' said Mum. 'We won't be a minute, Seán,' she said to Lisa's dad.

But when they came back, there was no sign of Maeve. They rushed over to where Dad was working with Samson.

'Is Maeve over here with you?' asked Lisa, looking around in a panic.

'No, love. Isn't she where you left her?'

'She's not!' said Lisa. 'She's gone! Oh no!'

'She can't have gone far,' said Dad.

But Lisa was really upset. She'd messed up before she'd even started! She and Dad went one way and Mum and Joe went the other.

'Don't worry,' Dad said, putting a hand on Lisa's shoulder, 'I bet–'

But he was interrupted by screams from the fashion tent. He took off in that direction. As they reached the tent, who appeared through the entrance but Maeve! Her front foot was stuck in a fancy shoe and there was a huge hat on her head.

Lisa's dad grabbed the calf and turned to face a large group of angry women.

'Sorry, ladies,' he said, 'it seems that our Maeve here thought she was in the Best Dressed Lady competition instead of the calf competition.' He quickly lifted Maeve's foot out of the shoe and Lisa handed the hat back to its owner, Geraldine, the vet.

Geraldine roared laughing. 'Good luck with this one,' she said, 'she's quite the supermodel!'

Lisa and Dad got Maeve back to the preparation area just in time. A few minutes later, the loud speaker announced the Heifer Calf Class B Category.

Lisa quickly combed the show wax through Maeve's hair, then wiped her hands and stood back.

'You look fab,' she said. 'Now, be good.'

Lisa and Maeve stood in line, waiting their turn. Finally, Lisa tugged on the halter, and they were on!

Lisa looked around the show ring. It seemed enormous. She and Maeve walked slowly around, then came to a stop in the middle. Maeve lifted her head proudly and stood perfectly still while the judges came over.

'So, who's this?' the first judge asked Lisa.

'This is Maeve,' Lisa replied. 'She's a Belgian Blue.'

'Very good. Did you train her yourself?'

'Yes, sir. But it wasn't too hard, she's a bit of a natural.'

'Is she, now? Likes to show off, does she?'

'She thinks she's a supermodel,' said Lisa.

The judge smiled. Then the judges examined Maeve carefully. And Maeve stood still the whole time!

At last the judges nodded and Lisa led Maeve to the side of the ring. Dad gave Lisa a thumbs-up.

Lisa had to wait while the other competitors had their turn. It was difficult holding Maeve, but finally the judging was over. The judges got together in a huddle. Lisa held her breath.

Then the main judge walked along the line and tapped the winning animals forward.

'In third place, Maurice Walsh with Caroline. In second place, Darragh O'Connor with Emer.'

Lisa could hardly believe it when her name was called.

'And in first place, Lisa O'Sullivan with Maeve.' He handed the red rosette to Lisa. 'Red for Maeve,' he laughed. 'She's a supermodel, all right!'

Everyone crowded around Lisa and Maeve, cheering. Her dad picked her up and gave her a massive hug.

'Well done, Missy,' he said, 'Maeve looks magnificent and you were a pro!'

Everyone started taking photos. There was even someone there from the *Farmers Journal*.

'You're going to be famous!' shrieked Niamh.

Lisa's dad opened a bottle of lemonade and they all had a toast:

'To Maeve – Glenmore's Next Top Calf-Model!'